WITHOUT SEPARATION

Prejudice, Segregation, and the Case of

Roberto Alvarez

LARRY DANE BRIMNER

ILLUSTRATED BY
MAYA GONZALEZ

CALKINS CREEK
AN IMPRINT OF BOYDS MILLS & KANE
New York

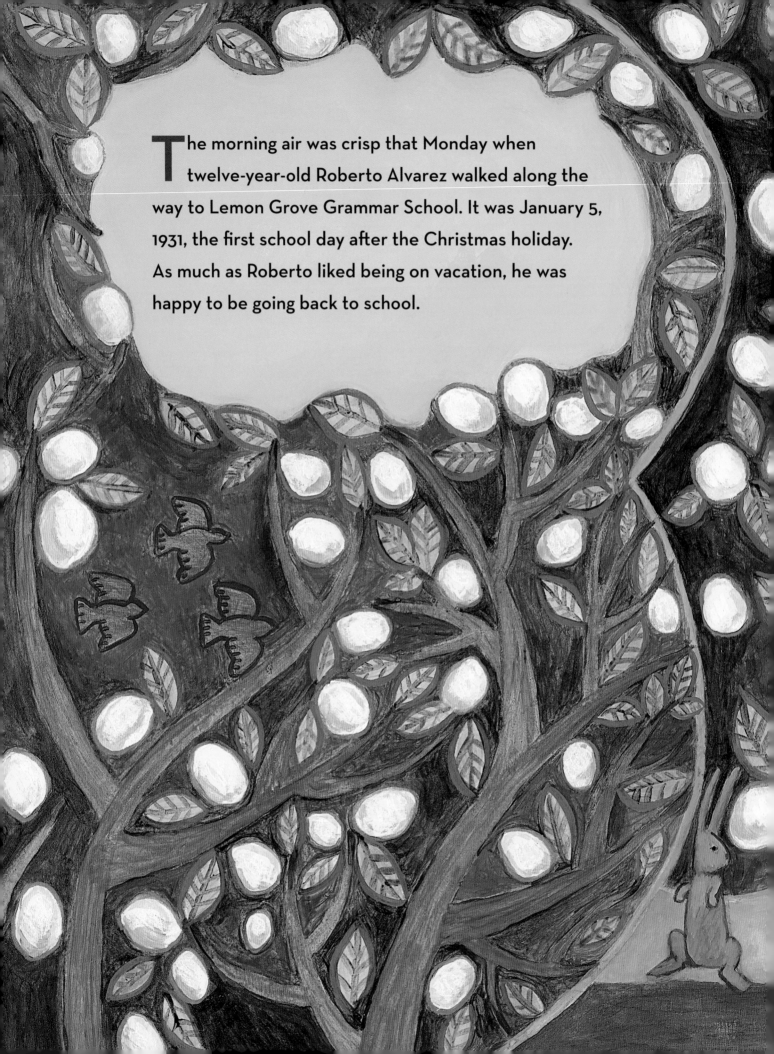

The morning air was crisp that Monday when twelve-year-old Roberto Alvarez walked along the way to Lemon Grove Grammar School. It was January 5, 1931, the first school day after the Christmas holiday. As much as Roberto liked being on vacation, he was happy to be going back to school.

Newspapers and the local chamber of commerce boasted that the rural community of Lemon Grove, just east of San Diego, California, had a modern, five-room stucco school. But that morning, as the school's principal greeted students, he didn't welcome them all.

The principal told Roberto and the other Mexican and Mexican American children that they did not belong there. He told them to go to the new school on Olive Street—the Mexican school. Their books and desks were already there. Their teachers were waiting.

Months earlier, on July 23, 1930, the president of the board of trustees of the school district had called a special emergency meeting to discuss a letter from the parent-teacher association. The letter said the Mexican children didn't understand English. This held back the white students. It complained that the Mexican children were unclean and endangered the health of every other student in the school. Something had to be done.

At another special meeting, on August 13, the board of trustees voted to construct a separate school for children like Roberto and his friends. But no one told the Mexican parents about it. To do so might lead to trouble.

Trouble came anyway.

Since work had begun on the two-room building on Olive Street, a rumor had circulated throughout the Mexican *barrio*, or neighborhood, that its real purpose was to segregate the Mexican children from the white pupils. When the principal told Roberto and the others to go to the Olive Street School, Roberto returned home instead. It was what his parents had instructed him to do if he was told to go to *la caballeriza*—the barnyard—which is what the grown-ups called the new wooden school building. Some seventy-four other students, nearly half of the entire school district's enrollment, joined Roberto in refusing to go to the new school. That January morning the Olive Street School stood almost empty, except for two teachers, three students, and many unoccupied desks.

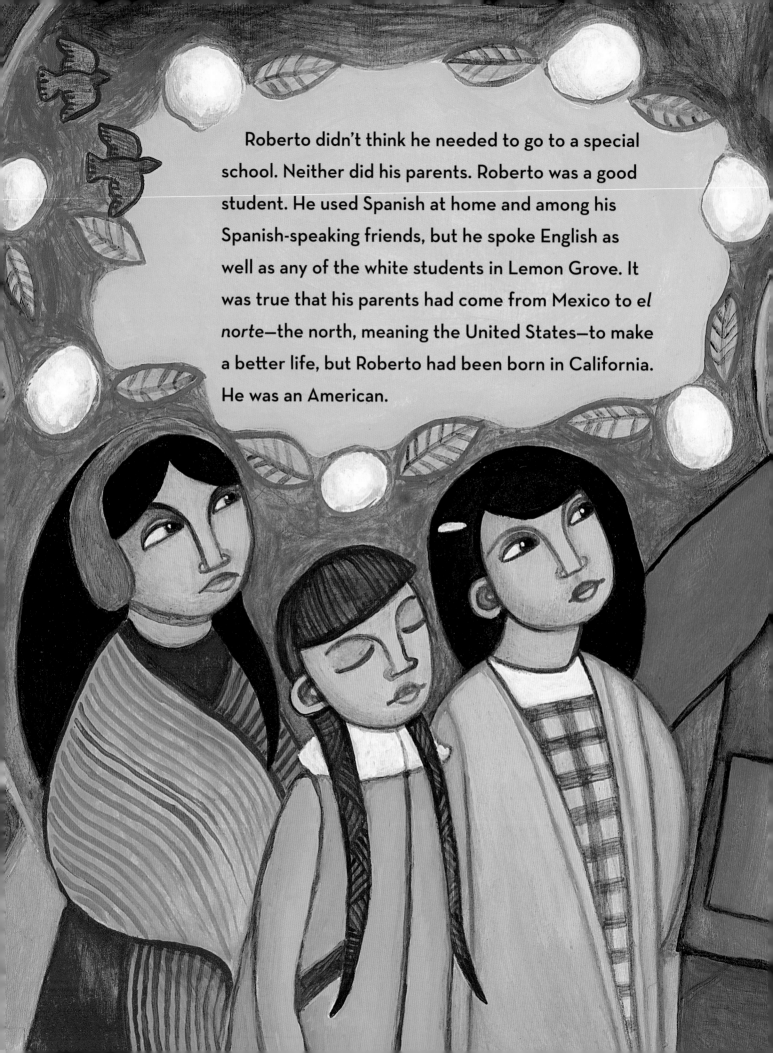

Roberto didn't think he needed to go to a special school. Neither did his parents. Roberto was a good student. He used Spanish at home and among his Spanish-speaking friends, but he spoke English as well as any of the white students in Lemon Grove. It was true that his parents had come from Mexico to *el norte*—the north, meaning the United States—to make a better life, but Roberto had been born in California. He was an American.

Roberto's mother and father joined other Mexican parents to form the Comité de Vecinos de Lemon Grove—the Lemon Grove Neighbors Committee. They held meetings in their homes to discuss what to do.

The new school was not meant to help their students learn the English language and American customs, as the school board and newspapers claimed. The only thing that determined which of Lemon Grove's two schools a youngster was to attend was the color of the child's skin, brown or white.

The parents met with the Mexican consul, an official of the Mexican government located in San Diego. He arranged for two local lawyers to help them.

Roberto brought the situation in Lemon Grove to the attention of the California Superior Court in San Diego on February 13, 1931. He filed a lawsuit against the board of trustees of the Lemon Grove School District. He asked the court to order the school district to stop discriminating against students like him. He wanted to attend the five-room school with white pupils as he and the other Mexican and Mexican American children had done before January 5.

The school board tried to sway the public by appealing to people's sense of Americanism, saying the strike by students and the approaching court case were organized by Mexico or by groups in Mexico.

Roberto and the other children knew it wasn't true. "It was the [Mexican] parents."

The president of the school board told a reporter that he welcomed the lawsuit. He knew San Diego's district attorney was on the school board's side and believed the court would order Roberto and the other Mexican and Mexican American children to attend the Olive Street School.

San Diego's district attorney represented the school board in papers filed with the court. He admitted that only three Mexican children had been attending the Olive Street School since it opened in January and called Mexican children "backward and deficient." The new school, he claimed, was not about segregation. It was for "better instruction."

But his words were at odds with the school board's minutes of the meeting held on August 13, 1930.

The district attorney added that the Olive Street School had been built out of concern for the children's safety—they would not have to cross the railroad track with a school in their own neighborhood. He asked the court to dismiss Roberto's lawsuit.

But Roberto wanted to be with his friends, brown and white. He asked the court for a speedy decision.

Roberto's case went to trial on March 10, 1931.
The trial was held at the courthouse in San
Diego. The school district officials insisted
that the purpose of the two-room school
on Olive Street was to benefit the Mexican
pupils. Again, they said it was not to separate

these children from Lemon Grove's white students. But Roberto's lawyers disagreed. They gave as evidence the minutes of the July and August school board meetings.

The trial ended on March 11.

What would the judge decide?

The judge, a justice of the Superior Court of California, reached his decision quickly. On March 12, he ruled that in the eyes of the law the Lemon Grove School District had no power to set up a separate school for Mexican children. Roberto had won—for himself and for all the other Mexican and Mexican American children living within the school district's boundaries.

Although the outcome of Roberto's case was known in March, it didn't become official until it was made public on April 16, 1931. The judge ordered the school board "to immediately admit and receive . . . Roberto Alvarez, and all other pupils of Mexican parentage" into the five-room Lemon Grove Grammar School "without separation or segregation." Under the law, they had a right to receive the same treatment, education, and instruction as that given to white students. They were entitled to equal education.

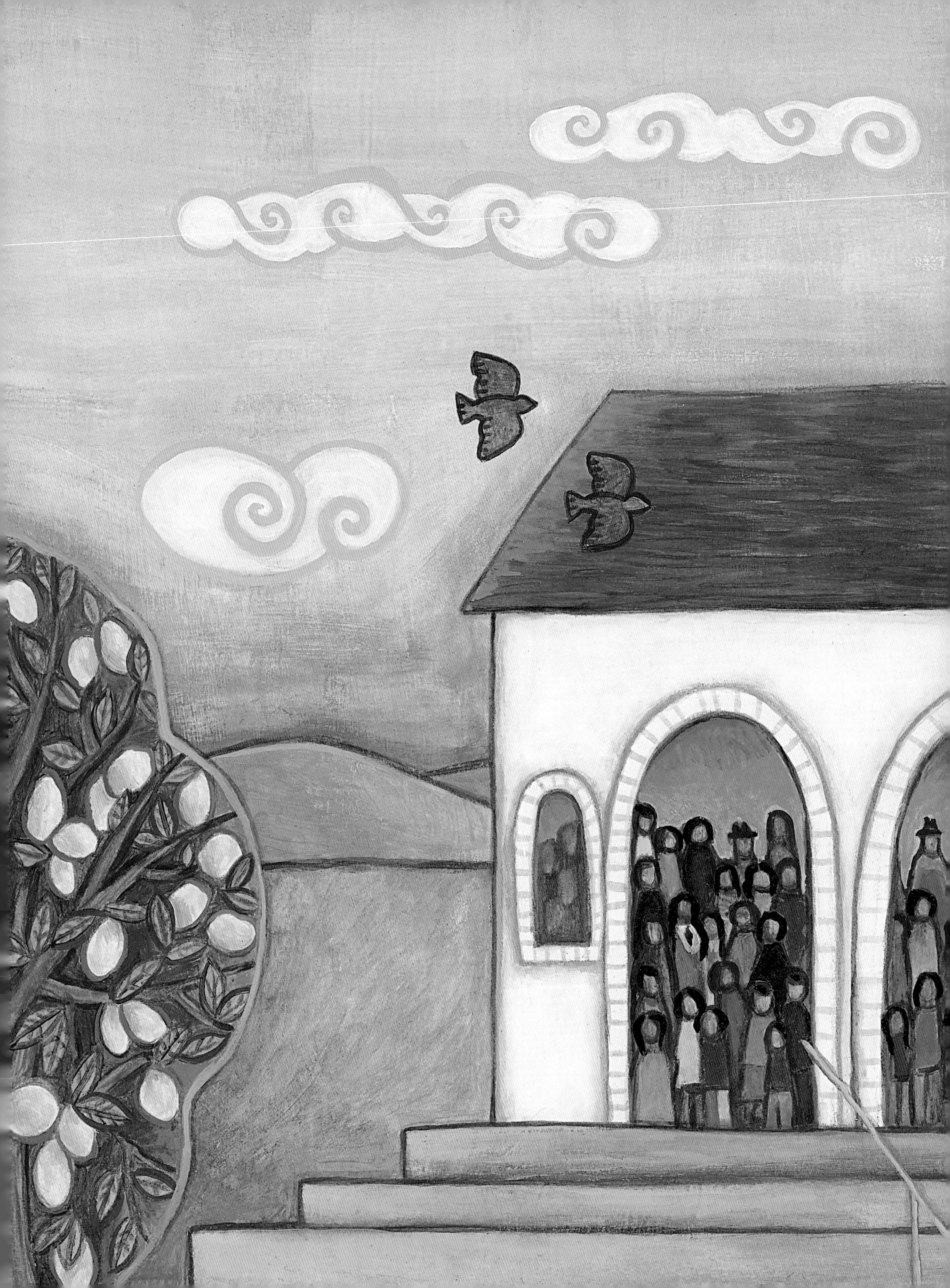

Sometimes a person has to stand up for what is right—
to fight for justice, to confront discrimination. Roberto
and his friends returned to Lemon Grove Grammar
School, and this time all were welcomed.

AUTHOR'S NOTE

Despite the Lemon Grove School Board alleging that the student boycott and lawsuit were brought about by the Mexican government or groups in Mexico, the children knew the truth. "It was the parents," David Ruiz said later. He had been one of the children turned away that January morning in 1931. In truth, the case of *Roberto Alvarez v. the Board of Trustees of the Lemon Grove School District* was initiated by the parents of the children who had been discriminated against. But instrumental in organizing them was Juan Gonzalez Sr.

Gonzalez came from Sonora, Mexico, where he had been active in workers' rights and knew Fred Noon, one of the two lawyers who would come to represent Roberto, from his labor activities there. Gonzalez had a large family, and many of his children also attended Lemon Grove Grammar School. He and Roberto's mother traveled to San Diego to meet with the Mexican consul, Enrique Ferreira. The consul had agreed that the situation was serious because this instance of segregation of Mexican and Mexican American students might lead to others. Young Roberto became the lead plaintiff and the case took on his name. Attorney Fred Noon needed to identify a child who had been turned away from the Lemon Grove Grammar School, one who was both a good student and fluent in English, in order to prove the school board's justification for the new school was false.

Roberto testified in court and was questioned by the judge. His responses were composed and showed a maturity beyond his youthful years. He and his brother stayed with an aunt in San Diego during the boycott and Roberto continued his education at Sherman Grammar School. We don't know the exact date the children returned to Lemon Grove Grammar School, but a *San Diego Sun* article dated March 12, 1931, indicated, "it was believed all would attend school today." Since March 12 fell on a Thursday, it is likely the students did not return until the following Monday, March 16. As for Roberto, his son, Roberto R. Alvarez Jr., indicated that he returned to Lemon Grove at some point during the 1931 school year. He graduated from Lemon Grove Grammar School in 1934.

Also, there is some confusion as to how many Mexican children made their way to the Lemon Grove Grammar School that January 1931 morning. Since the rumor was out that the Olive Street building was meant to segregate Mexicans and Mexican Americans, some believe a few parents kept their children at home. A small number of other families had moved out of the Lemon Grove area so their children might continue their education at schools that did not segregate. But court documents indicate that Roberto and a large group of children attempted to enter the five-room school and were denied entry. Nicolás Ceseña's three children also showed up and were turned away. Ceseña ran a tractor and plowing business and was fearful of losing customers if his children boycotted the Olive Street School.

Roberto Alvarez, third row, far left, with his third- and fourth-grade classmates in 1928. The identity of their teacher has been lost to time.

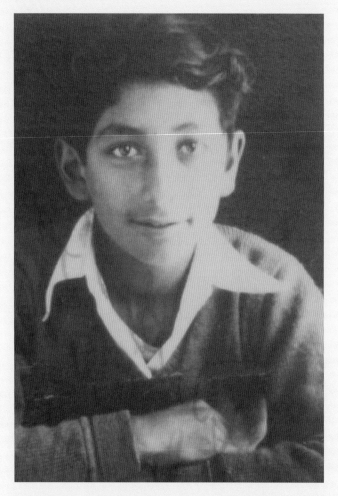

Roberto Alvarez's school photo, around 1930

Ramona Castellanos, the mother of Roberto, around 1925

His youngsters were the three who enrolled at the Olive Street School and were written about in local newspapers.

The Olive Street School was built at a time when many people were without jobs in the United States. It was the early days of the Great Depression, which eventually left millions of people homeless and without food. President Herbert Hoover and others blamed the bad times on immigrants, especially Mexicans. He accused them of taking jobs away from Americans. These accusations only served to create anger in many white Americans, some of whom called for people of Mexican descent to go back to Mexico, even if the only country they had ever known was the United States. America had been divided along racial lines since colonial times. The US Supreme Court upheld the constitutionality of segregation with its 1896 ruling in *Plessy v. Ferguson* that held separate facilities were legal as long as they were "equal."

Some two decades before the *Plessy* decision, however, the Supreme Court of California had legalized its own separate-but-equal policy in 1872, when the mother of Mary Frances Ward tried to enroll her eleven-year-old daughter at San Francisco's Broadway Grammar School, which had been reserved for white students. The principal, Noah F. Flood, had turned Mary away because she was African American and San Francisco had separate schools for black children. Mary's parents filed a lawsuit to end the segregation. The case was unsuccessful, but it did establish that if there was no separate school for Black children, then these young people had every right to attend school with their white peers.

Mary Frances Ward v. Noah F. Flood was followed by another attempt to desegregate San Francisco's schools, this time by a Chinese American. Chinese and Chinese American children had long been denied the right to attend San Francisco's public schools. The parents of eight-year-old Mamie Tape decided this was wrong and tried to enroll their daughter at their local school, Spring Valley Primary. The principal, Jennie Hurley, refused to admit her. In a case known as *Tape v. Hurley*, the Tapes filed suit in their daughter's name, charging Hurley and the school district of violating Mamie's constitutional rights. In March 1885, the California Supreme Court agreed, ruling that state law required public schools to be open to all children. But since the decision said nothing to reject California's policy of racially separate schools, the San Francisco School Board set about building a facility for the children of Chinese residents.

In California, as elsewhere in the western United States, the attitude about racial segregation resulted in so-called Americanization schools for nonwhite children. But these schools' real purpose was to separate by race or by color. This was true also for Native American youngsters like Alice Piper, a fifteen-year-old Paiute girl living in Big Pine, California. In 1923, Alice and six other young Native Americans petitioned to attend Big Pine High

School because it offered more educational opportunities than the local Indian school. California law, at the time, prohibited Native Americans from attending a public school if there was a government-run Indian school nearby. Piper's parents sued the school district on behalf of Alice, claiming the state law that had established separate schools for Indian children was unconstitutional. In its unanimous decision, the Supreme Court of California opened the doors for Native Americans to attend the state's public schools when it ruled in her favor in *Piper v. Big Pine* on June 2, 1924.

The *Alvarez* case was settled in Roberto's favor largely because it was against California law to establish segregated schools for Mexican students. While an early California statute had allowed for segregation of the "black," "red," and "yellow" races, as the law referred to African Americans, Native Americans, and Asians or Asian Americans, people of Mexican descent were considered Caucasian (white) and of European ancestry. Despite the *Alvarez* ruling, it wasn't until *Mendez v. Westminster School District of Orange County (California)* in 1947 that children of Mexican heritage legally won the right to attend school with their white peers throughout California. The *Piper, Alvarez,* and *Mendez* rulings were all cited as precedents before the US Supreme Court when it made its landmark *Brown v. Board of Education of Topeka (Kansas)* decision of 1954 that outlawed school segregation. *Roberto Alvarez v. the Board of Trustees of the Lemon Grove School District* is

Principal Jerome J. Green (sometimes spelled Greene)

Lemon Grove Grammar School

As the community of Lemon Grove grew in population, so did its only school. The wing to the main school was added between 1939 and 1941.

also important because it is recognized as the first successfully fought school desegregation case in the United States in which immigrants used the justice system to bring about change.

It should be noted that about seven children at the Lemon Grove Grammar School in 1931 were of Japanese parentage. They were not singled out to attend the Olive Street School.

The principal, Jerome J. Green, was fired when his contract with the Lemon Grove School District ended in 1931. He had opposed the notion of a special school for Mexican and Mexican American children from the outset and was at odds with the board of trustees. A special school wasn't necessary, especially given that the local chamber of commerce boasted that the school had "the highest scholastic standing of any elementary school in San Diego County."

Roberto Alvarez went on to found Coast Citrus Distributors in San Diego, which had two hundred employees and sales of more than one hundred million dollars in 1985. A philanthropist and civic leader, he passed away in 2003.

My hope with this book is that young people will learn about this significant event in United States history and understand that even one small voice can help bring about change for the positive. I also hope they will be able to connect the threads of the past with the intolerance that surrounds us today.

Roberto Alvarez, at Coast Citrus Distributors, around 1999

SOURCES CONSULTED BY THE AUTHOR*

TRANSCRIPTS

Superior Court of the State of California, County of San Diego. Case no. 66625. *Robert Alvarez v. E. L. Owen, Anna E. Wight, and Henry A. Anderson, members of and constituting the Board of Trustees of Lemon Grove School District, county of San Diego, California, and E. L. Owen, Anna E. Wight, and Henry A. Anderson, individually, and Jerome J. Greene.* [1931.] (Microfilm.) Primary Source.

Lemon Grove School District Board Minutes 1920–35. Lemon Grove Historical Society. (Transcript.) Primary Source.

FILM

Espinosa, Paul, producer and writer. *The Lemon Grove Incident*, DVD. Directed by Frank Christopher. San Diego, CA: Espinosa Productions, 1985. Release by KPBS TV. Available also at: "Lemon Grove Incident." YouTube video, 58:15. Posted by "Cha Cha Mal," on October 20, 2012. youtube.com/watch?v=Uu9dxMMLGyU. Quotations from the film are primary sources.

BOOKS

Alvarez, Robert R., Jr. *Familia: Migration and Adaptation in Baja and Alta California, 1800–1975*. Berkeley, CA: University of California Press, 1987.

Ofield, Helen M., and Pete Smith (Lemon Grove Historical Society). *Images of America: Lemon Grove*. Charleston, SC: Arcadia Publishing, 2010.

ARTICLES

Alvarez, Robert R. [Jr.]. "The California-Mexico Border and the Growth of a Mexican-American Community: A Regional Perspective." Teachers College, Columbia University (no date).

——. "The Lemon Grove Incident." *Journal of San Diego History* 32, no. 2 (Spring 1986).

——. "Reliving California: A Critical Look at California's Public History."

"Answer Made to Writ in School Row." *Evening Tribune* (San Diego), February 24, 1931. Primary Source.

Heyser, D. L. "My Mexican Friends and Lemon Grove's Segregated School, 1931." Memoir. Lemon Grove Historical Society. Primary Source.

Lemon Grove Chamber of Commerce. "Lemon Grove: Everything That Grows Can Be Grown Here." Advertisement. *San Diego Union*, January 1, 1931, p. 13. Primary Source.

"Lemon Grove School Strike Still Going On." *San Diego Sun*, February 11, 1931. Primary Source.

"Lemon Grove School War End Is Seen." *San Diego Sun*, March 12, 1931. Primary Source.

"Mexican Pupils Go on 'Strike' in Lemon Grove." *San Diego Union*, January 9, 1931. Primary Source.

"Orders Mexican Pupils Admitted at Lemon Grove." *San Diego Union*, March 12, 1931. Primary Source.

"S. D. School 'Strike' Reaches Court." *Evening Tribune* (San Diego), February 13, 1931. Primary Source.

"Seek to Compel School to Take Mexican Pupils." *San Diego Union*, February 14, 1931. Primary Source.

"75 Mexican Students Go on Strike." *Evening Tribune* (San Diego), January 9, 1931. Primary Source.

---

*Websites active at time of publication

Smith, Jeff. "Lemon Grove Incident (Part One)" Unforgettable: Long-Ago San Diego. *San Diego Reader*, p. 52, July 12, 2007.

Smith, Jeff. "Lemon Grove Incident (Part Two)" Unforgettable: Long-Ago San Diego. *San Diego Reader*, p. 38, July 26, 2007.

"'Strike' Is Ended at Alien School." *San Diego Union*, January 10, 1931. Primary Source.

"Trustees Reply to 'School' Suit." *San Diego Union*, February 25, 1931. Primary Source.

pp. 32–33: "It was believed all would attend school today.": "Lemon Grove School War End Is Seen," *San Diego Sun*, March 12, 1931.

pp. 36–37: "the highest scholastic standing of any elementary school in San Diego County.": "Lemon Grove, Everything That Grows Can Be Grown Here," Lemon Grove Chamber of Commerce, advertisement, *San Diego Union*, January 1, 1931, p. 13.

SOURCE NOTES

The source of each quotation in this book is found below. The citation indicates the first words of the quotation and its document source. The sources are listed either in the bibliography or below.

pp. 20–21: "It was the [Mexican] parents.": David Ruiz, quoted in Espinosa, *Lemon Grove Incident*, DVD, at 8:03.

pp. 22–23: "backward and deficient" and "better instruction.": Superior Court of California, no. 66625, Answer to Petition for Writ of Mandate, paragraph V [2].

pp. 28–29: "to immediately admit and receive… Roberto Alvarez, and all the other pupils of Mexican parentage": Superior Court of California, no. 66625, Judgment, April 16, 1931.

pp. 28–29: "without separation or segregation.": Ibid., p. 5, paragraph III.

pp. 32–33: "It was the parents.": David Ruiz, quoted in Expinosa, *Lemon Grove Incident*, DVD at 8:03.

ACKNOWLEDGMENTS

Many thanks to Roberto R. Alvarez, Professor Emeritus, Ethnic Studies, University of California, San Diego for his help with reviewing the text and art for *Without Separation*. Heartfelt thanks to Pam Muñoz Ryan and Helen M. Ofield. A special debt of gratitude is extended to the clerks of the Superior Court of California, San Diego, for ferreting out court records and transcripts from the 1931 trial.

PICTURE CREDITS

Lemon Grove Historical Society: 33, 36 (top, left), 36 (top, right), 36 (bottom)

Roberto R. Alvarez: 34 (top), 34 (bottom), 37

For Pam Muñoz Ryan—*LDB*

For all the courageous BIPOC families who believe
in their kids' future and work to transform the systems
that exclude and oppress—*MG*

Calkins Creek
An imprint of Boyds Mills & Kane, a division of Astra Publishing House
calkinscreekbooks.com
Printed in China

ISBN: 978-1-68437-195-2 (hc)
ISBN: 978-1-63592-460-2 (eBook)
Library of Congress Control Number: 2020947709

First edition
10 9 8 7 6 5 4 3 2 1

Designed by Barbara Grzeslo
The type is set in Neutraface Demi.
The illustrations are done in acrylic paint on archival paper.